DARK TALES
FROM THE WOODS

£10,00

DARK TALES
from the WOODS

DANIEL MORDEN
illustrated BRETT
by BRECKON

PONT

To The Company of Storytellers:
Ben, Pomme and Hugh
without whom . . . D.M.

Published in 2006 by Pont Books, an imprint of
Gomer Press, Llandysul, Ceredigion SA44 4JL

Second Impression – 2007

ISBN 9781843235835
A CIP record for this title is available from the British Library.

This book was first published with the financial support of the
Welsh Books Council.

Printed and bound in Wales at
Gomer Press, Llandysul, Ceredigion

Contents

Thanks and Acknowledgements   vi

Foreword   vii

The Squirrel and the Fox   1

The Leaves that Hung but Never Grew   19

The Fiery Dragon   30

The Master Thief   46

The King of the Herrings   55

Mary, Maid of the Mill   70

The Green Man   85

Thanks and Acknowledgements

I am very grateful to the following for their help in the preparation of this book: the National History Museum at St Fagans for their help in my research, and Teleri Jarman, a descendant of the Woods, for giving this project her blessing.

I would like to thank Academi for a bursary to support the writing of this book, as well as Gomer Press and the Welsh Books Council for the provision of a Literary Commission.

Foreword

'His complexion was very dark, with rosy cheeks. His face was as round as an apple and he had a double chin and a small mouth . . . He always rode on horseback, and would not sleep in the open, but in barns. He wore a three-cocked hat with gold lace, a silk coat with swallowtails – and a waistcoat embroidered with green leaves. The buttons on the coat were half crowns, those on the waistcoat shillings. His breeches were white, tied with silk ribbons, and there were bunches of ribbons at his knees. On his feet he had pumps with silver buckles and silver spurs, and he wore two gold rings, a gold watch and chain.'

Not much is known about Abram Wood, the great gypsy storyteller, described here by his great-granddaughter Saiforella. It is said he came to this country with his family at the beginning of the eighteenth century, bringing with him the first violin to be played in the whole of Wales. Many of his children and grandchildren and great-grandchildren became wonderful storytellers and musicians. One story says that Abram died in a cowshed on the slopes of Cader Idris, and that a great crowd followed his coffin to the graveyard, playing harps and fiddles all the way.

Two hundred years later many of the Wood family still made their living travelling Wales, performing to the local people, as I do today. It was then that a man named John Sampson took an interest in their stories and published them for the first time in a book. John Sampson's book has been out of print for many years, so I have chosen my favourite stories from it and told them in my own way.

The original versions are hard to understand. Here's an example:

> 'I go whither I go,' quoth Jack. 'Do thou remember to come here to these three crossroads in a year and a day; and if thou arrive before me wait for me, and if I arrive before thee I will wait for thee, if I be alive.'

I have made the language simpler and clearer. Sometimes the first half of a story was exciting, but the second half was told much too quickly. Sometimes a part of a story was missing. I have found versions of the same story in other books (such as the fairy tales by the Brothers Grimm) and used ideas from them to make my version more complete.

They are tremendous tales of enchantment, mystery and danger, where ordinary people have to overcome incredible obstacles. Often the heroes or heroines suffer terribly before they triumph.

Several of the tales are about one young lad. You'll already know Jack from his most famous adventures, *Jack and the Beanstalk* and *Jack the Giant Killer*. At the beginning of each adventure he is poor but happy. Jack isn't handsome or strong, but he is cunning, brave, and kind to those in need. Because of these qualities, he finishes each story rich, and married to the woman he loves.

These stories belong in the air, between a mouth and some ears. I hope that if you enjoy them, you'll have a go at telling them, or at least reading them aloud.

As Abram would have said,

That is all. Find out more if ye wish!

Best wishes
Daniel Morden

The Squirrel
and the Fox

Once upon a time, when squirrel and fox were still friends, two brothers lived in a village. One was called Jack. The other was called Tom. Jack was cheerful; Tom was not. Jack always had a quip on his lips. Tom could never think of anything to say. Tom was jealous of his brother. The people of the village called him Temper Tom. Jack made much more money than Tom, but whatever Jack had he spent at once. Tom made only a little money, but he was careful with it, and saved it.

It was New Year's Eve. The brothers decided to go a-travelling. Jack said to Tom, 'There is an old woman who lives in a cave near here. If we take her some bread and meat and beer, she'll tell us whether good fortune awaits us next year.'

Tom said, 'What does she know? We've little enough money as it is, without wasting it on her.'

'There's not much difference between one penny and no penny at all,' said Jack.

Off they went, taking whatever food they could afford.

In front of the old woman's cave they found a stone. They rolled it aside. Jack called, 'Grandmother, tell me of tomorrow. What is my fate?'

A little voice came from the darkness. 'Enter and I'll tell you.'

'I'm not going in there,' said Tom. 'What's the point?'

Jack went inside. The old woman was so ancient, she could no longer walk. Her face was a mass of wrinkles. It was hard to find her eyes and her mouth amongst the folds of mottled skin. Jack lit a fire to warm her and gave her what food and drink he'd brought.

He watched her eat. She squinted into the flames. 'I won't tell you what you want to hear. You want to hear only of good luck and gold. But that is not what I see. Shall I speak?'

Jack nodded.

'Here's a little stone for you. Keep it until you come to a crossroads. Spit on it and toss it in the air. If the golden side lands face up, take the right-hand road. If the black side is face up, take the left road. Take what you're given and make the most of it.'

Jack thanked her and returned to his brother. They set off. Eventually they came to a crossroads. The right-hand road led into the mountains. The left-hand road led to fields and farms. The road straight ahead led to a dark forest. Jack pulled out the stone. On one side it was yellow as gold. On the other it was black as coal. Jack spat on it and threw it into the air. It landed yellow side up. He told Tom what the old woman had said. 'We must take the right-hand road into the mountains,' said Jack.

'I told you she knew nothing! You want to follow the foam-flecked ranting of a mad woman. You wasted good food on her! There are fields and farms to the left. That means a chance to earn a crust. Up there, to the right, there'll be only wolves and bears. We'll split up. You go that way if you want. We'll meet again in a month!'

Off went Jack and off went Tom. Because Jack always had a quip on his lips, wherever he went he made friends. Whatever he turned his hand to made his pockets jingle.

When the month was up, Jack and Tom met at the crossroads. Each had a bulging sack.

'There you are!' said Tom. 'And look what I've made while you scrambled around in the hills!' Tom's sack was full of food.

Jack opened his sack. A light the colour of honey shone out.

'Gold! Where did you get all that?'

'Up there! The old woman was right! While you've been sweating, I've been singing. While you've been digging, I've been dancing!'

Tom stamped his foot and spat. 'Good old golden Jack! Handsome, happy, hero Jack!'

'Temper, temper, Tom! As soon as we find an inn, you know I'll give you a skinful.'

'That's it, waste the money just like you've wasted all the rest. With that gold we could go home and buy land!'

'I don't want land. I want adventure!'

Since Jack had travelled to the right, and Tom to the left, they had no choice but to go straight ahead into the forest. That forest was as silent as a church. No sound of brook or bird. Jack sang at the top of his voice, but soon the weight of the gold on his back stopped his singing.

The forest grew dark. The shadows stretched across the road. The brothers lit a fire. Jack said,

'I'm hungry. We haven't eaten a scrap since breakfast. My belly thinks my throat's been cut! Give me some food.'

'It's mine! Eat some of your lovely gold.'

Jack was amazed. He said, 'As soon as we reach a town, you can eat and drink at my expense!'

Tom snorted. 'Money and food mean nothing to you. You think they fall from the sky into your lap. Maybe they do for the likes of Jack, but they don't for me. Now you will learn what it feels like to be Tom. If you want to eat my food tonight, you'll have to pay for it. With half of your gold!'

'What do I care?' said Jack. 'Soon we'll find a town and I'll make more.' Jack ate his fill and handed over half of his hoard for the privilege.

Morning came. They walked all day with no sign of the forest's end. Jack was tired and weak. He said, 'My brother, I've been carrying this heavy load all day. I want to eat.'

Tom said, 'My brother, I'll give you food. And I'll help you with that load. Give me the rest of the gold and you can fill your belly.'

'How can you do such a thing?'

'I do it because you are my brother. It is time you learned the ways of the world. When I have what you need, I can ask as much as I want for it.'

'Take it! Tomorrow we'll be in a town and I'll make more.'

And he gave Tom the rest of his hoard.

They ate and then slept.

Morning came and no town appeared. They walked in sour silence. Tom ate his fill that evening, and gave Jack nothing. Jack had no money left to buy food. Another day, and another, passed in the same way. Jack was weak with hunger. He stumbled from one tree to the next. By the end of the day he could no longer walk. As they sat by the fire that night, Jack said, 'Brother, I have nothing to give you, and you have plenty to give me. Please, share the food.'

Tom said, 'I'm worried about you. I'm worried because you're my brother and you're nearly a man and still you don't know that you get nothing for nothing. If you want food then you must pay.'

'What with?' said Jack.

'If you want my food, you must give me your eyes.'

Jack was so shocked he could not speak.

'Did you hear me?' said Tom.

Jack had no choice. He was starving. He took out his eyes and gave them to his brother. Tom pressed some bread into Jack's hands in exchange. Jack ate his fill and then said, 'Tom,

please, I'm thirsty. Take me to a river. I can no longer see the way.'

There was no reply.

'Tom?'

Tom had gone. Jack was alone. He began to crawl on his hands and knees, calling for help. He crawled and crawled, until he had no idea whether it was day or night. His hands brushed against the bark of a tree. It began to rain. He found a hollow place in the trunk. He crawled in and lay down. 'This is a good place to die.'

Then from above him in the tree, Jack heard a shrill voice. 'Mr Tod! Oh, Mr Tod!'

A squirrel and a fox met in this place every twelvemonth, to tell stories and share the news.

A foxy voice outside answered, 'I'm here, Missus Fatcheeks.'

'Well then, Mr Tod, what's the gossip?'

'Have you heard about the princess?'

'Her in the city yonder?' said the squirrel. 'I hope she hasn't married. I'd hate to miss the wedding.'

'Hah! She'll never marry now,' said the fox. 'You see, last Wednesday she woke up, looked in the mirror and found a pair of horns had sprouted from her head overnight! Who's going to take a wife with horns?'

'A bull?' said the squirrel.

'She's a princess! She can't marry a bull!' said the fox, shaking his red head.

'The Prince of the Bulls then?'

'The Prince of the Bulls has already got a wife. A whole herd of the things!'

'You're right – they'd be jealous. She could marry a snail! Snails have got horns!'

'She can't marry a snail!' said the fox. 'Think of the palace carpets. Stop chattering and let me tell you the best part of my story! In the orchard of the palace there's a blood-orange tree. If she were only to eat one of those oranges, her horns would disappear overnight. I know that, you know that, but she don't know that!'

'Why don't you tell her then?' said the squirrel.

'Why should I? What has she ever done for me? Chased me up and down the valley, shouting, "Tally ho!" You get what you give, and she's given me nothing but trouble.'

'Fancy a nut?'

'No thanks, I just ate a nice plump duck. The city of the princess is in a right old state. Their wells have all dried up! They're having to go way down the valley every time they need a bucketful! If only they knew they could dig under their clock and get all the water they need! The best part is, I know that, you know that, but they don't know that!'

'That's right. Sorry, what did you just say?'

'I said,' snapped the fox, 'I know that, you know that . . . Oh, I don't know why I bother with you.'

'What else?'

'The mayor of the city has gone stone blind! And if he just rubbed a leaf from this tree against each eye, he'd get his sight back. But the best part is, I know that, you know that, but they don't know that!'

'Very good! . . .'

'Squirrel, what did I just say!'

'You said, if only the princess would dig under the orange duck, she could get water and go blind.'

The fox rolled his eyes and said, 'Go back to sleep!'

And they went their ways for another twelvemonth.

No more talk of dying for Jack! He felt the ground around himself until he held a leaf in each hand. He pressed them to his eyes. Tears poured down his cheeks, and with every trickling tear he saw more of the world around him. Soon he could see as well as ever he had done. Jack wept tears of joy. He picked up two more leaves and stuffed them in his pocket. He found the path again and, though he only had the strength to crawl, he followed it for an hour and came to a city. He croaked, 'Take me to the mayor! I am a great magician and I can cure the mayor!' The sight of him, a ragged, filthy traveller crawling on his hands and knees, caused many a man, many a woman, to turn away – but one of the mayor's servants, Siôn, was passing by. He heard Jack's words. The mayor was a kind man. Siôn loved him dearly, and had grown thin with worry over his master's plight.

'What harm can this beggar do?' thought Siôn. 'He can make no more misery than the doctors All their poking and prodding, all their potions and lotions only raised our hopes to dash them. What if this Jack really is a magician! It would be a miracle. If ever a man deserved a miracle, it is my master!'

So Siôn had Jack brought to the mansion, where he was led to the mayor's bedroom. Though he could see nothing, the mayor sat by the window. He loved to feel the heat of the sun on his face. His eyes were as white as milk.

Jack said, 'For my spell I will need good beef and chicken, cheese and ham and lamb, and bread and ale, and wine and cake – three kinds of cake!

11

And I must be left alone with the patient for the whole night!'

The food and drink were fetched. Once he was alone with the mayor, Jack pressed the leaves onto his eyes. Next morning the servant returned to find Jack and the mayor laughing and singing, surrounded by empty plates and bowls and bottles and jugs and cups.

'There you are!' shouted the mayor. 'I can see again, Siôn!'

Siôn cried tears of joy.

The mayor led Jack out into the square. The people of the city came out to meet their beloved mayor and his saviour. The news of Jack the Miraculous Magician spread across the city. The news reached the ears of Temper Tom. Oh, yes, Tom was in that same city, living off Jack's gold. And when he heard that Jack could see again – and had cured the mayor's blindness – Temper Tom felt a horrible twisting in his stomach, the old hatred of his handsome, clever, charming brother, who could be blinded and left alone in a forest one day and end up the hero of a city the next. The house Tom had bought and all of his gold seemed worthless beside Jack's effortless triumph. Wherever Tom went, he heard tales of Jack the Miraculous, the mayor's best friend, the greatest sorcerer the world had ever seen. Tom knew Jack was no sorcerer. Jack couldn't even read!

One day, as he sat in a noisy inn, listening to the story of Jack for the hundredth time, Tom suddenly said, 'Jack the Quack more like! If this Jack is so miraculous, if he is the greatest sorcerer the world has ever seen, surely he could heal the wells of this city! If he can restore sight to a blind man, he could find us water as quick as that!' Tom clicked his fingers.

The inn went quiet. A man murmured, 'That's right, he could.'

'Surely he could!' said another.

All around him Tom saw nodding heads, and he grinned. The rumour spread like a forest fire. Soon at every street corner, men and women were saying that Jack the Miraculous should heal the wells of the city. As it travelled from person to person, the rumour changed, as rumours do. It wasn't: Jack *should* heal the wells of the city; it was: Jack *would* heal the wells of the city. Then it was: Jack would heal the wells of the city *on Wednesday*. When Wednesday came, as Jack walked across the square, he was mobbed.

'There he is! Mighty sorcerer, we're here to see you perform your next miracle. Make the water come!'

'What?' said Jack.

'Mighty sorcerer, you said you'd heal the wells of the city!'

'Did I?'

'If you can heal the mayor's blindness, surely you can heal our wells!'

In the crowd, his face hidden by a hood, Tom smiled to himself.

Suddenly Jack shouted, 'Of course I can! Give me a rod of wood!'

Tom's face fell.

Jack whispered words and waved his hands over the stick. It jerked in his hands as though it had a life of its own. The stick pointed toward the town clock.

'Fetch spades! Fetch spades!' The people rushed to the base of the clock.

'Dig! Dig and your prayers will be answered!'

A great crowd gathered around Jack. More and more men and women joined in with the digging, some with spades, some with picks, some with their bare hands.

They uncovered a rock. They scraped away until they'd found its edges. A hundred hands lifted it out of the earth. There was a sudden sucking sound and a gush of fresh water swept them off their feet. Water enough for everyone! They cheered and threw their hats in the air. They cried tears of joy. Jack was carried through the streets.

Among the crowds there was Temper Tom. Jack had done it again! That night there were celebrations all over the city. Every inn was filled with laughter and song. Tom stood and scowled at the revellers. Someone said to him, 'Why the long face? We have water now! Jack has saved us!'

Tom said, 'This Jack is a great sorcerer. If he can heal the mayor's blindness and bring water to the city, surely he could banish the ugly horns that have grown on the princess's head!'

The rumour spread like a forest fire. First it was. Jack *should* heal the princess. Then it was: Jack *would* heal the princess. Then it was: Jack would heal the princess *on Wednesday*.

When Wednesday came, as Jack walked across the square, he was mobbed.

'There he is! Mighty sorcerer, we're here again to see you perform your next miracle!'

'Are you?' said Jack. 'Ah! Let me guess! You've come to see me banish the horns from the head of the princess!'

'Of course!' they said. In the crowd, his face hidden by a hood, Tom smiled to himself.

'Follow me!' said Jack.

A great cheer rose from the crowd. Tom's face

fell. Four soldiers lifted Jack onto their shoulders and took him to the palace.

The queen didn't like this charming rogue, but her daughter suffered so, and because Jack had performed two miracles, she reluctantly allowed him into the presence of the princess. The princess was a picture of misery. She was beautiful, except for the two enormous red horns that grew out of her forehead. Jack frowned and said, 'I thought as much. Bovine Pinnacle Boncitus. For my spell I will need good beef and chicken, cheese and ham and lamb, and bread and ale, and wine, and a blood-orange from the royal orchard. Oh, and cake – three kinds of cake! And I must be left alone with the patient for the whole night!'

'What?!' said the queen.

The food and drink were fetched. Next morning the queen returned and there were Jack and the princess, laughing and dancing, surrounded by empty plates and bowls and bottles and jugs and cups.

'Mother, look! Handsome, kind Jack has healed me! I've lost my horns and found my husband!'

'What?!' But there was nothing the queen could do. The rumour spread like a forest fire. In return for healing the princess, Jack was to marry her. The people were overjoyed. The palace was besieged with well-wishers. When would the wedding take place? Next Wednesday? Were commoners allowed to attend? Would the mayor be best man? The queen could no more stop the marriage than she could stop the sun sailing across the sky. She shed tears, but they weren't tears of joy.

Jack proclaimed that, as it was not right for princes to dirty their hands with spells, he would put aside his wizardry. The people said it was most noble of him to give up his incredible powers for the love of his wife.

It didn't take long for Temper Tom to get wind of the news. Jack the Miraculous was to become Prince Jack. Everywhere he turned, Tom saw pictures of his brother on banners and flags. Everywhere he went, he heard gossip about the wedding. And Tom felt that terrible twisting in his stomach. His fine house, his land, his herds of cattle meant nothing beside Jack's triumphs. And Tom had brought about all of those triumphs! Every one of Tom's traps had caused Jack more happiness. Tom could not bear to be in the city to hear the wedding bells ringing and watch the parade. He fled into the forest.

New Year's Eve came. Tom went to the crossroads. On one side he saw fields, on the other, mountains. He walked on until he came to a cave. He rolled the stone from the entrance. He called, 'Grandmother, tell me of tomorrow. What is my fate?'

A little voice came from the darkness. 'Enter and I'll tell you.'

Tom went in.

The Leaves that Hung
but Never Grew

There was once a weeping house.

The dog wept in the yard.

The master wept in the study.

Upstairs a young man sat at the end of his bed and wept. Day after day he sat, his right hand curled into a fist. He wept because he had forgotten everything. He wept for some awful misfortune he could no longer remember.

One evening a young lass walked up the drive.

Her clothes were no more than tatty rags.

She walked barefoot.

Her hair was clogged with twigs and leaves.

The dog paid her no heed. He lay whining in his muddy puddle.

The girl knocked at the door.

A sobbing servant fetched her in to see the master. He looked up from his weeping, dabbing his eyes with his handkerchief.

She said, 'I've heard tell of your son from the people of the village. I've heard tell that if any woman can make your son smile, she can have him. I will try. And if I fail, I don't know what I'll do.'

The master looked her up and down. Then he said, 'Many women have come here. Fine women, ladies, who wanted for nothing except a fine husband. They tried everything, singing, tickling, taking him into the sunshine, everything. All of them tried and failed. You have as much right to take your turn as those women. I wish you luck.'

The sobbing servant took her upstairs.

There sat the young man.

His face was grey.

There were grooves in his cheeks from all the tears he had cried. The servant had put a bucket under his chin.

The young woman began to speak. As she spoke, his tears plopped into the bucket.

'What cause have you to cry? You live here in this fine house. You have riches and servants. I have nothing, nothing in the world. My mother and father are dead. I have only the clothes I wear.

Listen to me now as I tell you a tale to pass the evening. Perhaps it'll stop one little tear.'

Once, not so long ago, a young woman called Anwen lived with her mother.

They were so poor they had to share a bed.

One night Anwen had a strange dream. She dreamed she should search until she found *the Leaves that Hung but Never Grew*. Next morning she told her mother about her dream.

Her mother sighed. 'If you've had a dream, you've had a dream. If you've set your heart on going a-travelling, I can't stop you. But be careful, my daughter. Sometimes the world is not as it seems. If you see something you don't understand, watch. Wait before you speak.'

Anwen kissed her mother and off she went. She walked and walked until one evening she came to a strange house.

Behind the house there was a hill.

On the hill there was a tree.

The tree was silhouetted against a red sky.

The tree had seven branches.

Each branch had one twig.

Each twig had one leaf.

Outside the house Anwen saw an old woman. 'Hello, my dear!' she said. 'Are you hungry? What

kind of a world would it be if I didn't have enough for one such as you! Come inside.'

Anwen said yes, she was hungry, and went in.

It was a strange place. Half of it was like any other home; the other half was a stinking pigsty.

Slobbering and snorting, chained in the corner, was an enormous black boar. It squealed and strained at its chain when it saw Anwen.

The old woman had a scrawny daughter. Anwen felt fat beside her. The old woman shouted, 'Bag-of-Bones! Make yourself useful! Put the kettle on the fire!'

The daughter flinched and scurried this way and that. The old woman threw a heavy serving spoon at her and it bounced off her back. But she smiled at Anwen and said, 'I bet you're exhausted. Sit down, please.'

Anwen sat and ate and drank.

She told the old woman she had nothing in the world, and that she'd set off to make her fortune. The old woman said, 'You can see I need an extra pair of hands here. My stupid, idle daughter couldn't boil a pot of water. I'll give you whatever I can spare if you can sweep the floor, keep the fire alight and feed the boar each night. We're fattening him up for slaughter next month.'

Anwen thanked her. She said she'd be glad to stay.

The days turned to weeks. Every day Anwen swept the floor, fed the boar and kept the fire alight. She lived well. The old woman gave her plenty of food and drink, and she insisted Anwen cleared her plate. For the first time there was flesh on Anwen's bones. But if ever her own daughter asked for a morsel more food, the old woman bounced a pot or a pan off her back. It was hard for Anwen to fill her belly while the spindly daughter of the house followed her every forkful.

Each evening Anwen would stare at the strange tree with its seven bony branches. But she was careful. She remembered her mother's advice and said never a word about it.

Until one day, while the old woman and her daughter were outside, as she fed the boar, she said, 'Months have gone by, and I don't know if I'm any closer to finding the leaves that hung but never grew. What should I do?'

The boar lifted its bristly head and answered! 'At last you have spoken to me. I had lost hope that you would ever do so! Now I can speak. Listen to me. The leaves on that tree are the leaves you seek! I was searching for them too. As a young man I came here and asked if I could have the leaves. She is a witch! She spelled me into a boar! Next month, when I'm nice and fat, they'll cut my throat and eat me. And guess who they'll spell next! You'll be a sow in this corner unless you steal those leaves and flee this place.'

That night Anwen crept outside and stole the magic leaves. With the first magic leaf she touched the boar and there was a fine young man before her.

With the second leaf she touched the poker, the broom and the chair. Then she and the young man fled.

Next morning the witch called to Anwen from her bed, 'My dear, what are you doing?'

The poker answered, 'I am raking the fire.'

So the witch rolled over and went back to sleep.

The witch woke up a second time and called again, 'My dear, what are you doing?'

The broom answered, 'I am sweeping the house.'

So the witch rolled over and went back to sleep.

Later still, the witch woke up again and called, 'My dear, what are you doing?'

The chair said, 'I am coming now.'

The witch waited. Anwen didn't come. The witch looked through her window. There were no leaves on her tree.

'Daughter! You miserable bag of bones! Anwen has freed the boar and stolen the leaves! Get after them! Get on the road and bring back whatever you find!'

Off went the daughter, running as swift as the wind. Anwen heard her coming. She took out the third leaf. 'We must hide. You'll be a pond and I will be a duck!'

Bag-of-Bones came to a duckpond. 'Little duck! Have you seen a young woman pass this way?'

But the duck dipped under the water.

Bag-of-Bones went home.

'Well?' said her mother.

'I saw nothing. Only a little duck in a pond.'

'That was them! Get me just one feather from that duck and I'll have them both in a blink!'

Bag-of-Bones ran back, but there was no duck, and no pond.

Off she went.

Anwen heard the witch's daughter chasing them, swift as the wind.

Soon she would catch them.

Anwen took out the fourth leaf. 'I'll be a rose, and you a bee.'

Bag-of-Bones came to a rosebush. 'Pretty bee, did you see a young woman pass this way?'

But the bee disappeared into the petals of the rose.

Bag-of-Bones went home.

'Well?' said her mother.

'I saw nothing, only a bee on a rose.'

'That was them! Get me just one petal from that rose and I'll have them both in a blink!'

Bag-of-Bones ran and ran . . . but she found no rose, no bee.

After them she went. Anwen could hear her gaining . . .

She took out the fifth leaf. 'You be a tree and I'll be an apple!'

Bag-of-Bones came to an apple tree. 'Sweet apple, did you see a young woman pass this way?'

But the apple only swayed on its stalk.

Bag-of-Bones went home.

'Well?'

'I saw nothing, only a red-cheeked apple on a tree.'

'That was them! Just one leaf from that tree and I'd have caught them both in a blink! If you want something done, you must do it yourself!'

She pushed her daughter aside and after them she went, as swift as thought.

Anwen heard the witch approaching. They came to a fork in the road. She gave the young man the sixth leaf and kept the seventh. She said, 'You go that way; I'll go this way. Meet me here in a week. If you get home, don't let anyone kiss you. If you are kissed, then you'll forget me immediately.'

The young woman ran to the left, the young man to the right. She looked over her shoulder, and there was a spidery grey hand reaching for her hair . . . she threw the leaf to the ground. The witch saw it and tried to turn her foot, but it was too late. She trod on the leaf and was changed into a sow.

Meanwhile the young man arrived at his home. His dog lifted her head and sniffed the air . . . joyfully she rushed toward her master. Before he could push her away, she jumped up and licked his face. In an instant he forgot everything.

His father saw him through the window and ran out and embraced his son. 'We thought you were dead. Where have you been?'

'I don't know where I've been. I don't know who I am. I can't remember anything.'

A week later, Anwen waited at the crossroads. No one came. She went home. As she approached the little hut where she lived, she saw no chickens in the yard. No smoke from the chimney. She opened the door.

Her mother was dead. Anwen buried her. Afterwards she couldn't bear to stay in that place. She took to wandering. She slept in barns and under hedges. She lived on berries and nuts. Her hair clogged into clumps. Her clothes became greasy rags. She was as bony as a whisper. She came to a village. An old man took pity on her, and gave her bread to eat and tea to drink. As she ate and drank, he told her all the gossip. She heard of a fine house where the young man had been struck down with a strange affliction. Once it had been a happy place. Now, even the pigeons on the gutters wept. The master of the house had proclaimed if any woman could make his son smile, she could have him.

Anwen went to the house and tried her luck.

The young man stared at her in amazement.
He smiled. He opened his hand.
She saw a leaf.

The Fiery Dragon

Jack was on the tramp, looking for work.

He came to a great hall. As he walked into the yard, didn't he see a young woman, the squire's daughter? She smiled at him.

'How do you do?' she said.

'How do you do?' said Jack, and smiled back.

They talked about this and they talked about that until the squire came out of the house. The squire saw Jack's raggedy clothes. He saw a vagabond giggling with his daughter.

'What do you want, you filthy, flea-bitten good-for-nothing?'

'I'm looking for work,' said Jack. 'I can do anything.'

'Oh yes?' said the squire. 'I bet you can't look after my cows.'

'Of course I can!' Jack was happy. If he had a job, he could stay and see the squire's daughter. He turned back to her, but she wasn't smiling: she was frowning.

That night Jack slept in the stable. Early next morning the squire's daughter came in to see him. She gave him a basket. 'Would you like something to eat?'

'Yes please,' said Jack.

What a feast! She gave him the finest ham, warm bread, good ale . . .

'Does your father know you've raided his larder?'

'Never mind that! Jack, you will be careful in the meadow today?'

'A few cows won't cause me any bother!'

The squire's daughter was about to reply when in came the squire himself. He saw the basket, the ham, the bread, the beer. He scowled at his daughter and said, 'Jack, the field you want is over the hill in the next valley. It is awful misty down there. A cow goes missing every day. Many a man has watched over them, but no one has caught the thief. You say you can do anything. Perhaps you'll have more luck than the others.'

Off went Jack with the basket. He led the cows

to the misty valley and settled down among them. Very soon his clothes were so damp from the mist that he was wet through. He lit a pipe. Something moved in the mist.

'It is a man,' thought Jack. 'But he must be a long way away, because he looks so very small.'

The man had a funny way of walking, almost waddling, swaying from side to side. As the man emerged from the mist, the pipe fell out of Jack's mouth. A dwarf!

'How do you do, sir?' said Jack.

'Middling, only middling, Jack. Hungry,' said the dwarf. He pointed at the basket and licked his lips. 'What's in there?'

'The finest ham, warm bread, good ale, given me by the squire's daughter. Tuck in!'

'Thank you kindly! I'll do that.' Jack didn't get a single scrap. The dwarf ate all the ham and all the bread and drank all the ale. He dabbed the crumbs from the bottom of the basket and licked them from his fingers. He shook the empty ale bottle over his open mouth. When he'd finished, he patted his tummy, belched, peered at Jack's pipe and said, 'I'll have a puff of that if I may.'

Jack handed him the pipe.

In one enormous suck all the tobacco was gone. The pipe was empty. He handed it back, let out an enormous cloud of smoke and said, 'Much obliged! Squire's daughter must have taken a liking to you to give you such a spread. Give her that when you see her.' It was a lovely ripe purple plum.

'Thanks!' Jack put it in his pocket. 'I thought she liked me, but she didn't like it much when the squire said I could keep an eye on the cows!'

'Ah,' said the dwarf. 'That's because the squire has sent you here, hoping you'd be gobbled up. Many a man has watched over the herd, but no one has ever stayed the whole day. They either run off or they're eaten.'

'Eaten!' said Jack. 'Who eats them? . . . You?'

The dwarf nearly split his sides with laughter. He doubled up and shook from head to foot. He rolled around in the damp grass until his hat fell off.

'No, Jack, the giant! Over there, hidden in the mist, is the giant's castle. Every day he eats one of the squire's cattle. If the cowherd puts up a fight, the giant eats the cowherd too. The giant is far too strong for you, but you could use your wits to overcome him. This is what you must do.'

And the dwarf told Jack how to kill the giant.

'Thanks!' said Jack, and he followed the dwarf's instructions. He stuffed a sack under his shirt, so the mouth of the sack was under his chin.

Jack walked through the mist until he saw the castle. Through the gates lumbered the most monstrous thing Jack had ever seen. A snaggle-toothed, stomping, vicious giant the size of a hill.

'Here comes my dinner! Maggot! Give me a laugh. Tell me why I shouldn't eat you!'

'I'm a giant too!'

The giant laughed. 'What? Look at you! You're no giant!'

'I am. I'm the smallest giant in the world.'

'Prove it. Do something giant.'

Jack picked a large mushroom. The giant squinted into the mist to see what he was doing. (Giants can smell and hear very well, but they have a poor sense of sight.)

'You see this stone?' said Jack. 'I'll crush it to gravel!'

Jack squeezed. The mushroom crumbled into bits and fell to the grass.

The giant gaped, then said, 'I can do better! Look!'

He grabbed a stone. He squeezed. He squeezed more . . . Nothing. He looked at Jack with admiration. 'Maybe you are a giant. Come inside and eat, my brother.'

Inside the castle there was an enormous pot squatting on the fire.

The giant ladled out two bowls full of porridge, each the size of a millpond.

'Porridge! Eat!'

Jack spooned all his porridge into the sack he'd hidden under his shirt. In a flash Jack's bowl was empty.

The giant watched in astonishment. He tried to keep up, but it was no use. Jack pushed away his bowl and said, 'More!'

'You want more?! You *are* a giant!'

The giant ladled out another bowlful for Jack, who shovelled the slop into the sack as quickly as he could.

'Don't you get full?' said the giant.

'After a while. I feel a bit full now, as a matter of fact. Give me that knife.'

The giant handed it over.

Jack stuck the blade through his shirt, into the sack and slashed sideways. The porridge poured out over his trousers. 'There, now there's plenty of room for more.'

'How did you do that?!'

'With the knife.'

'Didn't it hurt?'

'Just for a moment. When you eat, your belly is all food. I just cut through the flap of skin that keeps the food in.'

'Give me the knife!' The giant pushed the blade into his belly and slashed sideways. His guts poured out over his trousers. The giant went pale. He tried to push the guts back in, but it was no use. His head fell back and he was dead.

Jack searched the giant's castle. Inside the giant's stable he found:

a white horse,
a black horse
and a red horse.

In the armoury he found:

a white suit of armour,
a black suit of armour
and a red suit of armour,
a white sword and shield,
a black sword and shield
and a red sword and shield.

That night Jack returned to the squire's hall with all of the cattle. He said nothing about the dwarf, the giant and the castle. The squire counted the cows three times over. He was amazed.

'Give him whatever he wants!' said the squire,

and Jack ate his fill. Jack gave the squire's daughter the purple plum. She popped it in her mouth and said, 'Lovely!'

Every night Jack slept in the stable.

Every morning the squire's daughter came in with a basket. What a feast! The finest ham, warm bread, good ale . . . every day Jack thanked her, and they talked about this and they talked about that.

Every day Jack gave that basket full of food to the dwarf in the misty valley. Every day the dwarf gave Jack a plum which Jack gave to the squire's daughter.

One evening Jack returned to the hall to find the roof of the barn on fire. The farmhands were running this way and that with buckets of water. The squire's daughter was weeping and sobbing.

'What is the matter?' said Jack.

She said, 'While you were in the misty valley, a fiery dragon flew down from the sky and set fire to the barn. He said unless he could eat me tomorrow, he would blast the whole farm to ashes. Oh, Jack, would you stay here and protect me from the dragon?'

'Him? What can he do?' said the squire. 'We need a dragon slayer not a cowherd! Off with him down to the misty valley!'

So next morning, the squire's daughter gave Jack his basket. She said, 'This is my last day alive. Goodbye, Jack.'

They kissed and off he went.

When he reached the misty valley, Jack gave the dwarf the basket. The dwarf gave Jack a plum. The dwarf ate and ate until the basket was empty and said, 'Jack, what are you waiting for? I'll watch the cattle! Off with you!'

Jack rushed to the giant's castle, put on the white armour, the white helmet, took the white shield and the white sword. He went to the stable and climbed onto the white horse. It kicked the air with its hooves and galloped through the gates down to a river, and drank its fill.

In the yard outside the squire's hall, the squire's daughter was trembling from head to foot. Her father and all his men were watching from behind bolted doors. She saw a speck in the sky. The speck became a red smear. First it was the size of a bird. Then the size of a dog. Then the size of a cow. The size of an elephant. Now it was the size of a mountain.

The whole hall was in shadow. The air was black with a bitter smoke. The squire's daughter spluttered and gagged. The fiery dragon was over her now, scorching her face with its heat.

Its head was as big as a house. Its mouth was as big as a cave. Its every tooth was as sharp as a spear, its every claw as sharp as a sword. The nostrils were like trumpets. The eyes shone like stars. The sound of its wings was deafening thunder.

It swooped down to grab her – but into the yard came a white knight on horseback! The dragon spat a river of fire. The white horse spat a river of water in return and the fire of the dragon was doused. The fiery dragon roared, beat its leathery red wings and was gone into the sky.

When the smoke cleared, the squire's daughter found she was alone. There was no sign of the white knight.

That evening Jack returned with the cattle.

'Oh, Jack, I wish you could have seen it!' said the squire's daughter. 'A white knight came and saved me from the dragon! His steed doused the flames of the dragon's fire!'

'What did I say?' said the squire. 'We didn't need Jack; we needed a dragon slayer!'

Jack said nothing. He just gave the squire's daughter a plum. She popped it in her mouth. 'Delicious!'

Next morning, the squire's daughter brought Jack his basket of the finest ham, warm bread and good ale. Jack thanked her. They talked about this and they talked about that, then Jack took the cattle to the misty valley.

Jack gave the dwarf the basket and the dwarf gave Jack a plum.

'Jack, there's no time to waste! The dragon is returning!'

Jack left the dwarf with the cattle and rushed to the castle. On with the black armour. He grabbed the black shield and sword, onto the black horse and out to the river. The horse drank its fill.

Meanwhile, as the squire's men went about their business in the yard, the sky turned black. Above their heads there was the thunder of wings. They ran to the barns, shouting. The squire pushed his daughter out into the yard and bolted the door behind her. The heat of the fiery dragon burnt her skin. She screamed.

Then, out of the smoke came a black knight! He struck at the dragon with his sword. His black blade pierced its red hide. The dragon lunged at him, but the brave knight fended it off with his black shield. The dragon spat a river of fire. The black horse spat a river of water. The fire doused. The dragon roared, beat its leathery red wings and was gone into the sky.

The squire's daughter rubbed her eyes. There was no sign of her saviour.

That night, Jack returned with the cattle.

'I wish you could have seen it, Jack!' said the squire's daughter. 'A black knight wounded the fiery dragon!'

'Jack has no business watching dragons. His work is in the misty valley,' said the squire.

Jack said nothing. He just gave the squire's daughter a plum. She popped it in her mouth. 'Delicious!'

Next morning, the squire's daughter brought Jack his basket of the finest ham, warm bread and good ale. Jack thanked her. They talked about this and they talked about that. Then Jack took the cattle to the misty valley.

He gave the dwarf the basket and the dwarf gave him a plum.

'Jack, off you go!'

Jack left the dwarf with the cattle. On with the red armour, up with the red sword and shield, onto the red horse and down to the river. The red horse drank it dry.

Meanwhile, in the squire's yard the men were about their business. Anxiously they scanned the sky. One of them cried out and pointed. The fiery dragon was coming. They scattered. The squire pushed his daughter out into the yard, closed the door and bolted it behind her.

Down swooped the dragon – and into the yard came a red knight on a red horse! The red horse kicked the dragon with its sharp hooves. The knight struck the dragon with his red sword. The horse spat a river of water into the dragon's mouth. The knight struck again and again, until the dragon fell dead. All around the yard, doors burst open and men and women cheered. They clambered over the corpse of the dragon. The squire's daughter rushed to the red knight and embraced him. As she did so, she pulled a hair from his head. The red knight leapt onto his horse and was gone.

That night, Jack returned with the cattle.

'Oh, Jack, you should have seen it!' said the squire's daughter. 'The red knight killed the fiery dragon!'

'Never mind Jack,' said the squire to his daughter. 'We must find that noble knight and offer him your hand in marriage! I'll send messengers to all the nobles in the land. Tomorrow there'll be a wedding.'

Her eyes filled with tears. 'I don't want to marry a knight whose face I've never seen. I want to marry Jack!'

'What?' said the squire. 'You want to marry this scrawny, louse-riddled good-for-nothing when you could marry the man who killed a dragon and saved your life? Jack, be off with you to the stable before I set the dogs on you!'

Next morning, there she was in the stable, her eyes filled with tears. She gave Jack the basket. They kissed. Jack went down to the valley. He gave the dwarf the basket. The dwarf said, 'Today the yard will be full of noblemen wanting to win the hand of the squire's daughter. This is what you must do.'

Jack followed his instructions.

Sure enough, a great host of knights and princes and lords gathered in the yard outside the squire's hall. The squire saw Jack among them. 'What are you doing here?' shouted the squire. 'Didn't I tell you to watch the cattle?'

The squire's daughter ran forward. In her hand she had the hair she'd pulled from the head of the red knight. 'If all these other men are allowed to try their luck, why isn't Jack?' She sat down and Jack put his head on her lap. She compared the hair in her hand against the hair on Jack's head. They were identical.

'You can't marry him! You are promised to the red knight!' shouted the squire. Jack pulled off his filthy jacket and shirt. The red armour shone out from beneath. Into the yard galloped the red horse. Such cheering and shouting! The squire had no choice but to consent. Jack took the hand of the squire's daughter. What a wedding they had! There was dancing and laughter for seven days and seven nights. Even the dwarf had enough to eat!

Jack and his wife went to live in the giant's castle. They live happily even now: I was there last week.

The Master Thief

There was once an old couple who'd worked hard all their lives. They'd paid their rent on time, gone to church each Sunday and doffed their hats to the lord of the manor. They died shivering in their shack, wrapped in one another's arms.

The people of the village, even the lord of the manor, Lord Bateman himself, came to their grave to say farewell. As the mourners stood in the wind, a carriage and four came along the path. Out of the carriage stepped a fine gentleman dressed all in black.

He took off his hat and bowed his head.

Lord Bateman, curious, greeted the gentleman. He gestured to the grave. ''Tis a pity. These two were model tenants. I never had any trouble from them. They were decent people with good manners. Always on time with their rent.'

'What happened to them?' asked the stranger.

'The harvest failed. They froze to death.'

'Did they not have any offspring to care for them in their old age?'

'They had a son – he was my godson – but what a child. He was nothing like his parents. A wayward rogue who wouldn't be told. He fled from here as soon as he could.'

'Would you know him if you saw him?' asked the stranger.

'I'd know him by the birthmark on his hand. But why speak of him? He didn't even come to his parents' funeral. I should think he's rotting in prison somewhere,' said the lord.

The gentleman took off one of his gloves. There was the mark.

Lord Bateman gasped. 'You've come too late. You should never have left. You should have stayed with your parents.'

'If I had, all three of us would be cold in the ground now. That miserable patch of land couldn't feed me as well as them.'

The lord looked at his fine clothes. 'I see that you have made your fortune. What trade did you learn?'

47

'I am a thief.'

The lord was outraged. 'A thief? A common thief? What kind of a trade is that?'

'An ancient trade, practised by kings and counts and noblemen. And I am not a common thief. I am a master thief. I am a better thief than you. You took so much from my parents that they starved. You killed the goose that laid your eggs. If you'd let them off their rent for one month, you could have had their money for another ten years.'

'Watch your tongue, you vagabond!' said Lord Bateman. 'I could have you slung in prison.'

'I am a master thief. For me there are neither locks nor bolts. And I'm no vagabond. I steal only from those who deserve my attentions. Such as you.'

Lord Bateman went pale. 'You would not dare to steal from me!'

'Name anything, anything in your possession, and I will steal it from you.'

'Because you are my godson, I'll show you mercy. If you can steal my horse, the sheet from my bed and the wedding ring from my wife's finger, I'll grant you are a master thief and I'll give you an amnesty. But if you fail, my men will hunt you down and you'll be fruit on the gallows tree.'

They shook hands. The lord went home to warn

his servants, but the thief went ahead in secret and was watching from behind a bush when Lord Bateman arrived.

The lord summoned one of his servants. The poor man was dressed in rags. He was paid so little he couldn't afford a decent pair of boots to keep out the cold. He shivered as he listened to his master.

'I met a thief today. I bet him that he couldn't steal my horse. I want you to take the beast to my brother's house. Make sure you lead it carefully – if I catch you sitting on its back, you'll be flogged. Is that clear?'

The servant nodded.

Bateman went back into his home.

Straightaway, the thief was off to market. He bought a pair of boots and he ran to the road the servant would be taking. The thief laid one of the boots by the side of the road.

He ran a little further on and laid down the other boot.

Then he climbed a tree and hid.

Behind him, the servant led the horse along the road. Before long he stopped. 'Look at that! A fine boot!' He tried it on. 'About my size too.' He looked around. 'But what use is it without the other?'

He left it there and walked on.

After a mile he came upon the second boot. 'Blow me! There is the other! What a fool I was not to take the first one! I only hope it's still lying back there.' He tied up the horse, turned around and ran. Once the servant was out of sight, the thief jumped from the tree onto the horse, untied the reins and he was off.

That night the servant returned with a brand new pair of boots but no horse. Lord Bateman was about to accuse him of selling one to buy the other when into the courtyard, astride Bateman's horse, galloped the grinning thief.

He said, 'Don't blame your servant. If you paid him a little more, perhaps he wouldn't neglect his work to see to his comfort.'

Bateman smiled with his mouth but not with his eyes. 'You'll remember that this was not the sum of the bargain. You have to steal my wife's wedding ring and the sheet from my bed. You will marry the rope-maker's daughter yet.'

That night Bateman entered his bedroom with a loaded rifle.

'Are you bringing that to bed?' said his wife.

'I am,' he replied, 'and not a word from you!'

She sighed and rolled over.

In the meantime the thief went to a gallows and cut down a dead man who was hanging there. He waited until all was silent and crept to the manor house. He put a ladder under Lord Bateman's bedroom window and pushed the body up the ladder. Bateman saw the shape of a head appear at his window. He took aim, and fired.

The thief let go of the body and it tumbled to the ground. He heard the lord cry out with glee. 'Got him!'

The thief scrambled down the ladder and hid in the garden.

When Bateman went to look, he saw a body on the ground. Cackling to himself, he summoned his servants. 'Fetch spades,' he said. 'Dig a hole in the woods and bury the body!'

Bateman went back to put on his clothes.

'What are you doing?' said his wife.

'I'm going to watch,' he replied.

She rolled over and muttered, 'You should be ashamed of yourself.'

Once the servants were out of the house, the thief went in, straight to the lord's bedroom.

The wife awoke from her slumber. Half asleep in the dark, she saw the shape of a man enter. 'What has happened?' she said.

The thief spoke in the voice of Lord Bateman. 'That rogue is dead . . . but he was my godson after all. As I saw him lying there, suddenly I knew you were right. I was ashamed. I remembered him as an innocent child before he went wrong. I cannot help feeling some pity for him. For the sake of the child he was, I think we should give him the ring and the sheet. He sacrificed his life for them. It is the least that we can do to bury them with him.'

'Oh, husband, what a kind thought,' she said, giving him both ring and sheet.

The thief made off at once.

Eventually once the burying was over, Bateman returned to his home, exhausted. He crept into bed and fell asleep.

Next morning, when he awoke, he looked at his wife and said, 'I see no ring on your finger, nor sheet on our bed. No doubt you hid them for fear of that rogue.'

'I did no such thing. I gave them to you! You buried them with him!'

'I did what?!'

At lunchtime the thief arrived at the manor house with ring and sheet.

Bateman said through gritted teeth, 'I was wrong. You are not a common thief. You are, as you claim, a master thief. You have outwitted me and mine at every turn. You are a danger to the respectable folk of this land. I swear by God I'll see you swing!'

The thief grinned. 'Tut tut! Don't you remember our pact? We agreed if I could steal your horse, your wife's ring and the sheet from your bed, then I would be granted an amnesty. We shook hands! Respectable folk keep their promises! Folk who don't keep their promises are called rogues!'

The lord said nothing. Trembling with fury, he nodded.

The thief bowed, and walked away, never to be seen again.

That is all.

The King of the Herrings

A quarryman and his wife loved each other well. All their lives they'd prayed for a child, but it was only when they were very old that their prayers were answered. The wife was frail and white-haired when her belly began to swell. The neighbours were amazed that so old a woman could bear a child.

A life for a life, they say, and so it was with mother and son. At the moment of the baby's birth, his mother died, and the quarryman had to rear the baby himself. He did the best he could, but he was old, and his son was young. The quarryman was afraid that he would die before his boy became a man and could look after himself. His worst fear came true. What with earning a crust and caring for his child, the quarryman became so tired he took sick and died.

The quarryman's son was called Jack. As he walked away from the funeral, Jack found himself lost in a thick mist. He heard a voice at his ear.

'Do you need help?'

Jack looked around. He could see no one, but the voice was familiar to him and made him feel less alone. He answered, 'Yes, I do.'

'What kind of help do you need?'

'I need a companion. Just a bow-legged, scabby, shaggy nag to be by my side. A nag, to cheer me when I am low, to help me when I despair, to carry me to the end of the earth.'

'Your wish is granted.'

Out of the mist before him came a bow-legged, scabby, shaggy nag.

It spoke! 'Climb onto my back and we'll be off!'

Jack climbed onto its back and off they went, so swiftly the breath was gone from his body.

'Where are we going?' said Jack.

'Where you said – to the end of the earth.'

'What must I do?' said Jack.

'If you meet anyone in trouble, you should help them all you can. And leave whatever you find.

Don't touch it, even if it is the finest thing you ever saw. It'll be trouble for you.'

The world sped by in a blur. Jack couldn't tell if the nag's hooves touched the earth at all.

They crossed a beach. Jack shouted, 'Stop! I hear something!'

The nag stopped. Jack jumped down and searched the beach. He found a flipping, flopping fish, a herring that the tide had left stranded.

Jack picked it up at once and put it back into the sea. The herring lifted its head to the surface and said, 'Oh, Jack, I thank you. You saved my life. When you need my help, call for the King of the Herrings and I will come!'

'I will!'

Jack shook the reins of the nag and they were off. Fields and farms and forests sped by in a blur. The wild wind roared in their ears. They passed a vast castle on a hill. Jack said, 'I hear something!'

The nag stopped. Jack slid off its back and climbed the hill. There was an awful moaning. He ran through the castle gates and into a courtyard. Jack scrambled up a huge flight of stairs. Each one was the height of a man.

He came to an enormous doorway and went in. He found a giant lying on a bed. The giant said,

'Oh, Jack, I'm sick and all alone. Fetch me food, I beg you!'

Jack scrambled down the stairs and brought the giant food and drink from the kitchen. The giant ate his fill.

'I thank you. You saved my life! When you need my help, call for the King of the Giants and I will come!'

'I will!'

As Jack passed though the gates, something blew into his mouth. He picked it out and threw it away. It blew in again, and again. Jack grabbed it and looked: it was a feather from a golden bird. Jack's clothes were rags; his shoes were patched; his horse was a nag – he'd never owned anything fine or new. This feather was perfect and beautiful. It shone like the sun. It was the finest thing he'd ever seen. He couldn't bring himself to part with it, so he put it in his pocket. Down the hill he went, and onto the nag, without another word.

They travelled through the night until they came to the city. As Jack climbed down from his nag, the feather fell from his pocket.

'What's that?' said the nag.

'Just a feather. On the hill I found a feather from a golden bird.'

The nag hissed, 'Oh, Jack, what did I say? I told you to leave it! This feather will cause us trouble. Put it away at once!'

Jack put it back in his pocket, but it was too late. One of the king's servants had seen it. He went straight to his master.

'Your Highness, I have just seen such a wonder! The finest thing I ever saw. A young man had a golden feather that shone like the sun!'

'Bring him to me!' said the king. Jack was brought to the palace.

'Give me that feather!' Reluctantly Jack gave it to the king. He glared at it, then glared at Jack. 'You brought me the feather – bring me the bird!'

'Your Highness, the feather came on the wind! I have never seen or heard of the bird. It could be anywhere in the wide world!'

'You will bring me the bird or I will cut off your head!'

A guard pressed a sharp sword against Jack's throat. Jack bowed, turned and left.

He went down to the stables. There was his nag, munching straw. One look at Jack told him that something was wrong.

'What's the matter?' said the nag.

Jack sighed and said, 'I wish I had listened to you. The feather has brought trouble. The king took one look at it and demanded I fetch him the bird it came from!'

'What did I tell you?' said the nag. 'But don't worry; I'll help you all I can. Ask the king for three days and three purses of gold.'

Off went Jack and his nag, far, farther than far, to the end of the earth, over the surface of a vast ocean, making not a ripple, until Jack saw something glittering on the horizon. He said, 'Is that the sun?'

The nag replied, 'It is the palace of the Princess of the Sun. The golden bird belongs to her. She keeps it in her bedroom. An army watches over the princess. But don't worry about them. They're all asleep. Take the bird, touch nothing else and we'll be away before they wake.'

They reached the gates of the palace. Jack dismounted and crept through. Sure enough, the courtyard was strewn with sleeping soldiers. Jack picked his way between them. He searched golden room after golden room, until he came to the bedchamber of the Princess of the Sun. There was the golden bird in a cage at the window – but Jack barely looked at it, because before the cage there was a bed, and in the bed slept the Princess of the Sun. He had thought the feather perfect, but now it seemed a tawdry twig beside the beauty of the princess. He feasted on her beauty. He loved her with all of his heart the moment he laid eyes on her. Her hair was the colour of shining summer. She wore a bewitching smile even as she slept.

A single stray hair had fallen from her head onto the pillow.

'I'll never see the princess again,' he thought. 'What harm would there be in taking one little hair for a keepsake?' Carefully he lifted the hair . . . but once it was off the pillow, the princess jerked upright and screamed. Jack grabbed the cage with the golden bird and ran, stumbling over stirring soldiers, who shouted and grabbed at his clothes. He bounded into the courtyard and onto the nag. As the nag leapt over soldier after soldier, Jack risked a look back. He wished he hadn't! The princess and her entire army were just behind him, shouting and lunging at the nag's tail. The nag jumped through the palace gates and kicked them shut. The soldiers fell over one another in their attempts to open the gates. The nag was on the ocean and out of reach in a moment.

Back to the king went Jack. He gave the king the golden bird.

'So soon?' said the king. 'Was it far away?'

'Farther than far, across a vast ocean, in the palace of the Princess of the Sun.'

'I've heard of her. Tell me of the Princess of the Sun.'

'I've never seen anyone so beautiful, Your Highness.'

'Then she will be my bride. You will bring me the Princess of the Sun!'

'But, Your Highness . . .'

'You will bring me the Princess of the Sun or I will cut off your head!'

A guard pressed a sharp sword against Jack's throat. Jack bowed, turned and left.

He went to the stables and wept.

'What is the matter?' said the nag.

'Oh, my friend, I wish I had listened to you. I wish I had given the feather to the wind. The king ordered me to bring him the Princess of the Sun!'

'Don't weep. I will help you all I can. Go back to him and ask him for three days and three bags of gold.' Off went Jack and nag again. When they came to the vast ocean, the nag said, 'Wish I was a ship laden with silk.'

No sooner had Jack whispered the words than the nag became a fine galleon, whose holds were full of bright silk. The sailors bowed as Jack climbed aboard. The sails bulged and they were off, far, farther than far, to the end of the earth. The guards on the battlements of the palace of the

Princess of the Sun saw the wonderful ship approach. They sent out a soldier to discover what business the ship had in those waters.

'Silks!' shouted a sailor. 'We have brought fine silks for the Princess of the Sun!' And with that, he hoisted seven flags of bright silk up a mast. The princess came to the battlements. She loved bright things. Never had she seen such fine silk before! She went to the shore. A rowing boat took her out to the galleon. A sailor led her down into the hold . . . as she inspected the cloths she felt the ship shift . . . she ran on deck and saw that the palace had sunk beneath the horizon. She saw Jack on the deck and her eyes blazed.

'Oh, Jack, why have you stolen me away?'

'I had to. If I hadn't, the king would have cut off my head!'

'Would you have me marry your fat old king?'

She pulled out of her pocket a bunch of keys and threw them over the side. The sea became as red as blood. The sky became as black as oil. White waves battered against the boat. The rest of the voyage was a battle with wind and wave.

When the king saw the princess, he beamed.

'Ah, my bride!' He held out his hand, but she did not take it.

'What is the matter?'

'I want to be in my palace, not yours!'

'What?' said the king. He blinked, then turned to Jack.

'You brought me the princess – you bring me her palace!'

'Your Highness . . .'

'You will bring me her palace or I will cut off your head!'

A guard pressed a sharp sword against Jack's throat.

Jack looked at the princess. She shrugged. He bowed his head, turned and left. He went straight to the stables. The nag only had to look at him a moment and he knew something was wrong.

'What does the king want?'

'He wants the palace of the princess!'

'Don't weep. I will help you all I can. Go back to him and ask him for three days and three bags of gold.' Off went Jack and nag, but they hadn't gone far when Jack said, 'Dear nag, you've made a mistake! This is the wrong way! The sea is to the west, and we ride to the east!'

'Trust me,' said the nag, and soon they came to a castle Jack knew.

'King of the Giants!' shouted Jack. 'If ever I needed your help, it is now!'

Out of the castle came the King of the Giants. He strode across the sea as if it was a puddle, pushed his fingers under the earth and wrenched up the palace of the Princess of the Sun, the soldiers running and shaking their fists. He waded back across the sea and dumped the palace beside the city of the king.

'This is all very well,' said the princess, 'but I can't enter my palace without my keys. And I dropped them into the ocean.'

'Jack,' said the king. 'You brought me the palace – you bring me the keys!'

'But, Your Highness . . .'

'You bring me the keys or I will cut off your head!'

A guard pressed a sharp sword against Jack's throat.

Jack looked at the princess and she smiled, as if to say, *what can I do?*

Jack bowed his head, turned and went to the stables.

'What now?' said the nag.

'The king wants the keys the princess threw to the bottom of the ocean!'

The nag laughed. 'Oh, Jack, don't you remember the King of the Herrings?' The nag took him to the sea. As soon as Jack called, the water bubbled and there was the King of the Herrings. He disappeared into the dark depths and returned within the hour with the keys in his mouth.

'Thank you!' shouted Jack as he rode away.

'Thank you for saving my life!'

Jack took the keys to the princess. She looked at them. She looked at Jack. She looked at the king. She unlocked the gates, and out of her palace came hundreds of shining soldiers. A shining sergeant shouted, 'Give us back the princess or we will burn this city to the ground!'

The king's guards had no choice. They were outnumbered. The guards dropped their weapons. The princess said to the king, 'Your Highness, do you love me?'

'Of course I do,' said the king. 'You are beautiful.'

She turned to Jack. 'Jack, do you love me?'

'I have loved you ever since I saw you sleeping in your palace.'

The king glared at Jack.

The princess said, 'If I am to spend my life with a husband, then I must know how much he loves me. Your Highness, who do you love above all others?'

'Myself!' said the king.

'Quite true. Jack, who do you love above all else?'

'My nag.'

'Quite true. Your Highness, would you give your life for me?'

'Of course not!'

'Jack, would you kill your nag for me?'

'He would!' It was the nag that spoke.

'I would not!' said Jack.

'If you kill your horse, then you will have proved how much you love me. You will have proved that you love me more than the king does, and I will marry you and spend my life with you. A life for a life.'

Jack's eyes prickled with tears. He put his face to his horse's muzzle.

'Jack, listen to me,' whispered the nag. 'Think back over our adventures. When you listened to me, all went well. When you ignored my advice, remember what happened. Listen to me now when I tell you that you must cut off my head.'

Jack slowly drew his sword and lifted it aloft. He took it in both hands. He shut his eyes as he brought it down. He felt the sword strike the nag's neck. He opened his eyes. The nag lay dead. Tears fell down Jack's cheeks.

'You have won me,' said the princess and she took his hand.

The king had to accept. The shining army of the Princess of the Sun surrounded him.

Jack heard the voice of the nag in his ear.

'Jack, don't weep for me. Do you remember when we first met? After my funeral? Jack, I am the spirit of your father. You asked for a faithful companion, to cheer you when you were low, to help you when you despaired, to take you to the end of the earth. I was that companion for as long as you needed me. You are a grown man now, so I will go to Heaven where I belong.'

Mary, Maid of the Mill

There once lived a young lass named Mary. She wasn't what they call beautiful, but she had her wits about her. She lived with her parents in a mill outside town. Her father's mill did well. She didn't want for much, and she could do most of anything around the place. Because she wasn't what they call beautiful, she never got invited to the local dances. She never complained. She kept busy.

But one summer, there was a young man who came to buy flour. Handsome he was, well dressed too. Whenever he smiled at her, she found she was blushing. The young man's name was Caley. He got on well enough with her father. He said he was a steward for a fine gentleman.

One time Caley said to Mary, 'Not far from here in a fine house there's to be a masked ball. Maybe I could take you.'

'Maybe you could. Where do you live?'

'Not far. Just the other side of the forest, with my mother and my brothers.'

The following week, while Caley was at the mill, Mary's father got a letter. It said he had to visit his uncle, who was at death's door.

'Me and your mother should see him one last time. Would you keep the place while we're off? Only open the gates to those you know.'

He turned to Caley. 'Next week it'll be my daughter who'll look after you.'

'Very good.' Caley smiled at Mary and she blushed.

On Sunday night her father put on his hat and her mother put on her bonnet, and off they went on their cart.

All through Monday, whenever Mary heard a noise, she'd rush to the window. At last, that evening, along came Caley in a wagon with four barrels.

'Mary, can I ask you a favour? You see, I'm fetching these for my master. It's too late to go home now. I'll have to rent a room at the inn. But if I take these down to town tonight, by the morning they'll be gone. Could I leave them in your yard? I'll be back for them, and the flour, in the morning.'

'Of course,' said Mary.

So Caley lifted the barrels from the wagon and rolled them to a corner of the yard.

That night Mary locked the gates of the yard, locked all the doors from the yard to the house, and climbed the stairs to her room.

It was hot, so very hot she couldn't sleep. From her bed she could see the yard, the shapes of the barrels in the shadows down below. So she lay there watching them, thinking of Caley.

After some time, she saw the lid of one of the barrels shift. She rubbed her eyes and looked again. To her horror she saw the lid lift off the top of the barrel, and a shadow emerge. The thief made for the kitchen door.

Mary was so afraid, she couldn't swallow. She'd locked the door, but because of the heat of the evening, she'd left the kitchen window open.

Mary wasn't what they'd call beautiful, but she had her wits about her. And some would say in the end it is better to be clever than beautiful. Down the stairs she went, into the kitchen. She picked up a knife. She stood with her back to the wall, the door to her right and the window to her left. She saw the door handle turning, turning. She saw hands at the window. She heard the grind of the sash lifting. The shape of a head came through the gap. With one hand she covered the man's mouth and with the other she thrust the knife into his body. She pulled the robber through the gap until he lay still on the kitchen floor.

As his black blood welled out across the tiles, Mary saw something glinting against his cloak. She knelt beside the corpse and found a chain. On the chain there was a whistle. She looked at it, and then she looked at the other three barrels. She dragged the corpse away from the window. Then she blew the whistle once.

The lid of the second barrel lifted. Out came the second robber, and through the window . . . It was the same with him. Soon he lay twitching beside his companion. The same with the next, and the next . . .

When the four barrels were empty and the kitchen floor was covered with corpses, Mary took a long knife from one of the robbers. She crept across the yard to the gate. She drew the bolt across and opened it. Straightaway, a man stepped through. She knew the swagger. It was Caley, the man she'd so admired, charming, cunning Caley.

She lunged at him with the knife. He gasped and cursed and drew his blade. Mary was clever, but Caley was quick, and skilful, and a knife is no match for a sword. She shouted, 'Come and get him!'

Thinking that Mary was not alone, Caley fled. After all, how could one woman have killed four men?

Mary heard the sound of a horse galloping away. She searched the yard. In the moonlight she saw something at her feet. She knelt and picked it up. It was one of Caley's fingers. She'd cut it off. She put it in a barrel, fetched the keys, locked the gates and set off after him.

On the ground she found spatters of black blood. They led her to the forest. Further and further she went, into the woods, following the black spatters.

She heard a horse approaching. Maybe Caley had seen her, turned his horse about and was coming for her. All at once Mary was terrified, and she hid.

But it wasn't Caley who came down the path. It was an old woman wrapped in a black cloak, riding on a grey mare. Mary stepped out onto the path and told her story.

'Where was I that dreadful night?
Lying in my bed so wide.
Along comes a fox with a smile so bright,
A band of cutthroats by his side.
The wind did blow, my heart did quake
To see the holes my knife did make.'

When Mary'd finished, the old woman shook her head. 'Well, you're a rare one and no mistake! Listen to me now. You've done your part. Much more! What are you thinking of, running into the forest after a thief and a murderer?'

Suddenly Mary could see herself, a young woman, dressed only in a filthy, blood covered nightdress, far from safety. Suddenly she was tired, and hungry, and thirsty.

The old woman said, 'The constable will find that rogue. We'll go to the town at once. You come along with me. Climb up here.'

Mary climbed onto the horse in front of her. The old woman gave Mary a drink from her bottle and wrapped her cloak around Mary's shoulders. She put her hands around Mary's waist, grabbed the reins and off they went.

The horse broke into a gallop. Faster and faster it went.

'Is the town much further?' said Mary.

'We're not going to town. If I were you I wouldn't be in a hurry to get where we're going.'

'You're Mother Caley!'

'I'm Mother Caley. My son sent me to catch you. We're going to my house, where there'll be four empty beds tonight. You killed four of my sons. Four spare beds, but you'll not sleep in them. My only living son is digging you a bed!'

Something squatted in the dark ahead, something low and broad. A mud hut.

Mother Caley bundled her in. There was Caley, pacing, his hand bandaged. He grabbed Mary and tore off her shoes. He dragged her into the next room and tied her by her hair to the roof beam.

'Any screaming and it'll be the worse for you in the morning!'

And off he went.

Mary looked about herself. On the straw-covered floor she saw a piece of cracked pot. She curled her toes around it and picked it up. With that shard she cut through her hair, strand by strand, and freed herself.

With that sharp shard she scraped at the mud wall until she'd made a hole. She squeezed through. She stumbled in the dark, and tumbled into a pit. She tried to climb out, but the earth was so fresh, the sides of the pit came away in her hand. She found a root and used it to pull herself up. She crawled on her hands and knees until her hand fastened on a branch, a branch sticking out of the damp earth. She felt up the branch, hand over hand . . . and found a bonnet dangling off the top.

The moon came out from behind a cloud. She looked about her. The branch was a grave marker. There was another grave beside it. And another, and another . . . She was surrounded by graves. And she had stumbled and fallen into her own.

Each marker had a hat or bonnet dangling off it. Some of them were no more than sodden filthy rags; some were brand new. Mary saw nearby her father's hat and her mother's bonnet.

Suddenly she heard the scream of a fox. Someone was coming. She ran to a tree and climbed it, the bark scratching her skin. She clambered onto a branch and squatted there, above the leaves, clinging to the trunk, barely daring to breathe. She could see two dark shapes below.

'What was that?' It was old Mother Caley. 'I swear I heard something in that tree.'

Poor Mary was trembling from head to foot. They were standing under her now, Mother Caley and her savage son. Mary prayed to God that the leaves would hide her, and clouds would hide the

light of the moon. She heard him draw his sword from his sheath. He thrust it up among the leaves. She felt it slice the flesh of her left heel. She felt piercing pain as the blade broke her skin. Though she'd never before suffered such a sting, she kept her head. She clenched her teeth and made not a sound. Hot blood trickled from her foot. It dripped onto Caley's face.

'It's started raining,' he said to his mother. 'This is hopeless. We can't see nothing. It can't be long until dawn.' And they were gone.

A tear squeezed from Mary's eye, down her filthy cheeks and onto the leaves. She got down from the tree. She made off in the direction of the thickest thickets, so they couldn't follow on horseback. It was hard for her, running through the brambles and briars, stumbling shoeless and with a bleeding foot. She heard the sound of a wagon and horses. She hid herself but the wagon stopped and a man cried, 'You there! If you're a living Christian, come out. If you're a ghost, be off with you!'

She knew the voice. It was an old man who lived in the town. He had an apple orchard. Sure enough, the wagon was full of apples. The old man gaped at the state of Mary, pulled off his coat and put it around her. She told her story.

'Where was I that dreadful night?
Lying in my bed so wide.
Along comes a fox with a smile so bright,
A band of cutthroats by his side.
The wind did blow, my heart did quake
To see the holes my knife did make.

'I ran to the woods for to find Mr Fox
But old Mother Vixen caught my scent.
He bound me tight by my own flowing locks
But into the bitter night I went.
The wind did blow, my heart did break
To see the hole that fox did make.'

'Help me,' cried Mary. 'They're searching for me!'

'Under the apples with you!' The old man scooped them apart. She lay on her back in the cart and he piled the apples over her.

Meanwhile Mother Caley and her sly son had reached home. When they lit a lantern, she saw dried blood on his cheek. 'That blood ain't yours. Mary must have been in that tree!'

Not far away Mary peeked out from under the apples. The touch of bright dawn was on the dark sky. She heard galloping. She felt the cart come to a stop. She heard Caley's voice. 'Old man, have you seen a pretty young woman come this way?'

'A what?!' said the old man. 'I can't say I have, more's the pity.'

'Are you sure?'

'I think I'd have remembered. Come to think of it, I saw a flash of white down that track by the stream a few miles back.'

'That was her!' Caley shook the reins and was gone. The old man cackled and set off again.

Soon Mary heard the sound of the horse once more.

'You lied to me! I checked the ground. No barefoot bleeding woman walked that track!'

'I didn't tell you no lies!' said the old man. 'I said I saw a flash of white. It was you as said it must have been the woman.'

'What have you got in the wagon?' said Caley.

'What does it look like? Apples.'

Mary heard Caley climb down from the horse and draw his sword.

'Watch out!' said the old man. 'An apple cut into pieces is worth nothing!'

'The same could be said of a man,' said Caley. The whole cart shuddered as he stabbed into the apples once, twice . . . then Mary heard another horse approaching.

It was Mother Caley. 'We know where Mary's going, and she's on foot. We'll reach the mill before her. Let's wait for her there.'

Off went mother and son together.

The old man took Mary to his home. He sheltered her there for weeks, telling no one except the constable.

Then one Friday, in a fine house nearby, there was a masked ball.

All the fine young men and women were there, dressed in strange and wonderful costumes. Some came as pirates, some as kings and queens, or wild beasts. All of them hid their faces. The hall was filled with drinking and laughter.

The time came when each one of them should tell a tale, or a riddle, or a song. Amongst them there was a dandy of a fellow dressed as a fox. He was quick and clever. He had a flattering verse or a charming riddle for every pretty maid. There was quite a crowd about him, enjoying his wit.

'What about a song?'

The fox turned to see who had spoken. He beheld a young woman dressed all in black.

'A song?' he said. 'My Lady, haven't you heard us firebrushes sing at night? It isn't a sound for ears such as yours. But blackbirds such as yourself sing as sweet as honey. Give us your song.'

'A riddle first,' she replied.

'Too small for a horse, too large for a bee,
This door is opened with never a key.'

'Hmn!' he said. 'Is it a mouth?'

'Not a mouth.'

'Tell us then.'

'Too small for a horse, too large for a bee,
This door is opened with never a key,
Sure 'twas the grave you dug for me.'

The fox stopped smiling. He looked about himself. 'Oh, no. Not so,' he said.

'You don't like my riddle? A song, then.

'Where was I that dreadful night?
Lying in my bed so wide.
Along comes a fox with a smile so bright,
A band of cutthroats by his side.
The wind did blow, my heart did quake
To see the holes my knife did make.

'I ran to the woods for to find Mr Fox
But old Mother Vixen caught my scent.
He bound me tight by my own flowing locks
But into the bitter night I went.

The wind did blow, my heart did break
To see the hole that fox did make.

'Doors that were opened with never a key,
Two led to Heaven and four led to Hell.
Still there's a door that you made for me –
You left it wide open so you'll use it yourself.
The wind will blow, the bough will shake
And then, by God, your neck will break!'

'Oh, no. Not so,' he said.

'It was so, and here's the proof I have to show!' And she held up, for all to see, the finger she'd cut from his hand when they'd fought. The young men fell upon him, grabbed him and pulled off his gloves. A finger was missing from his left hand. Caley cursed and threw off his captors. He leapt out of a window but the constable was waiting below. Caley was caught and hung from a gallows tree. He was buried in the hole he'd dug for Mary.

What became of his mother? I cannot say.

The Green Man

Once there lived a lad called Jack. He was a charmer, a Jack-the-Lad and a master card player. Men would come from the four corners of the country to challenge him. They always went away with empty pockets.

One winter evening there was a knock at Jack's door. Before him stood a fine gentleman.

His clothes were as green as ivy.

His eyes were as green as jet.

His teeth were as green as moss.

His skin was as green as grass.

His long green hair spilled over his shoulder.

'I've heard tell from many a man that you are the finest cardsharp in the world,' said the gentleman. 'I'll put you to the test. If you win, you can have anything you ask for. Anything.'

They settled down to play. Jack beat the gentleman easily.

The gentleman scowled. 'What do you want?'

'You said anything,' said Jack. 'I want you to build me a castle.'

'Is that all? Look.'

Jack looked out of the window. There was a magnificent castle. The gentleman laughed. 'You could have had anything. A bag of endless gold, the water of life, eternal youth, and you chose a draughty damp castle.'

'Would you play again?' said Jack.

'I'll play again, but only by my rules. If you win, you can have anything you want. If I win, I can have anything I want.'

'Good!' said Jack.

This time the gentleman won easily. 'You remember our bargain!' he said. 'I can have anything I want. I want you. I am the Green Man Who Lives in No Man's Land. You must find my castle within a year. If you fail, I'll cut off your head!'

Suddenly Jack was alone. Not a wink of sleep did he have that night.

Next morning Jack set off on his horse, searching for the Green Man's castle.

The days became weeks.

The weeks became months.

Five, six, seven, eight, nine, ten, eleven months went by.

Jack had many adventures. He travelled the length of the country. From Narberth to Barmouth. From Sirhowy to Abertawe. From Caernarfon to Camarthen. Over wild mountains and through dark forests. Many times he risked his life. He battled bandits and bears, wolves and witches and triumphed over them all. At the moment of victory, instead of heaving a sigh of relief, he'd remember the green gentleman and Jack's heart would pound against his chest.

One night the snow was deep on the ground.

Jack was far from any village, far from any town.

He saw a light in the darkness.

He saw a cottage with a flat roof.

He went to the door.

A white-haired, trembling old woman welcomed him and offered him shelter. That night he slept in front of her fire. Next morning the old woman said, 'You're a long way from anywhere. What brings you here?'

'I'm looking for the Green Man of No Man's Land!'

'Hmn!' she said. 'Never have I heard of such a one. Come with me.'

She led him outside. She took out a ladder. She stood it against the wall, climbed onto the flat roof and blew a horn so loud, all the trees Jack could see leaned in the blast.

There was a great thundering of feet. All the people of the world stood before them. The old woman shouted, 'Have you seen or heard of the Green Man of No Man's Land?'

The people of the world frowned.

First they scratched their heads. Then they shook their heads.

A woman cried out, 'There are folk here from Snowdonia, Caledonia and Patagonia. From Bangor, Bankok and Bangalore, Aberthaw, Arkansas and Abbey Dore. But none of us has ever heard of the Green Man of No Man's Land.'

'Begone!' said the old woman.

A thundering of feet and she and Jack were alone again.

She shrugged. 'I'm sorry, I can't help you. But ask my big sister down the road! She is much older than I am. Take my horse and throw this ball of thread between his ears. Don't hold the reins. Let him take you where he will.'

Jack got on the horse. He threw the thread

between his ears and whoosh! The horse was off and the breath was gone from Jack's body.

They came to a cottage. A very old woman opened the door. She was so old she was bent double. 'It is a long time since I saw my little sister's horse!' she said. 'Come in!'

Once again Jack slept the night in front of the fire.

Next morning the very old woman said, 'You're a very long way from anywhere. What brings you here?'

'I'm looking for the Green Man of No Man's Land!'

'Hmn!' she said. 'Never have I heard of such a one. Come with me.'

She led him outside. She took out a ladder. She stood the ladder against the wall, climbed onto the flat roof and blew a horn so loud, all the trees bent double.

He heard a thundering of hooves, and suddenly all the animals of the world were there.

Pugs, slugs and firebugs.

Frogs, dogs and hedgehogs.

Wombats, dingbats and meerkats.

The very old woman shouted, 'Have any of you heard of the Green Man of No Man's Land?'

They scratched their heads. Then they shook their heads.

A pig snorted, 'There are beasts here from Gotland, Rutland and Jutland, Arran, Saron and Tregaron, Aberidw to Mogadishu. But none of us has ever heard of the Green Man of No Man's Land.'

'Begone!' said the very old woman.

A thundering of hooves and they were alone.

'Sorry, I can't help you. Ask my big sister down the road. She's much older than I am. Take my horse. Throw this ball of thread between his ears. Don't touch the reins. Let him take you where he will.'

So Jack climbed on the back of the horse, threw the ball of thread and off he went. At last he reached a cottage. Out came an ancient woman, so old she was bent over so far, her nose made a trench in the earth like a plough.

'It is a long time since I saw my middle sister's horse!' she said. 'Come in!'

Jack slept the night in front of the fire. Next morning the ancient woman said, 'You're a very long way from anywhere. What brings you here?'

'I'm looking for the Green Man of No Man's Land!'

'Hmn!' she said. 'Never have I heard of such a one. Come with me.'

She led him outside. She took out a ladder. She stood it against the wall. She climbed onto the flat roof and blew a horn so loud, all the leaves on the trees flew away.

Jack heard a beating of wings, and all the flying things of the world were there.

Bats, gnats, woodchats,

Horseflies, houseflies, flutterbyes,

Bees, fleas and chickadees.

All the flying things of the world except one. Jack could see no eagle.

The ancient woman shouted, 'Have any of you heard of the Green Man of No Man's Land?'

Much scratching of heads. Much shaking of heads.

'There are creatures here from Chile, Scilly and Caerphilly, Paris, Treharris and Beaumaris, Epsom, Hexham and Wrexham. And none of us has ever heard of the Green Man of No Man's Land.'

'Begone!' said the ancient woman.

A tremendous flapping of feathers and the sky was empty.

'Wait, Jack! Look!' said the ancient woman.

There was a scar against the sky. It grew and grew until Jack saw it was an eagle.

The ancient woman said, 'Have *you* heard of the Green Man of No Man's Land?'

'I have, though I wish I hadn't!' said the eagle. 'He is a powerful sorcerer. He has lived for thousands of years. No one knows how he can be killed. I am his slave. I guard an egg for him in No Man's Land. If he finds out I am here, he'll cut off my head.'

'Tell me where he is,' said the ancient woman.

The eagle whispered in her ear and then flew away as quickly as it could.

'Take my horse,' said the ancient woman. 'Throw this ball of thread between his ears. Don't touch the reins. Let him take you to No Man's Land. You'll come to a great lake. Hide yourself and the horse. Three swans will come. They will fly to the shore and shake off their feathers. Then you'll see them as three sisters. They are the daughters of the Green Man. While they're bathing, steal a feather. The woman who owns the feather will beg you to return it. Don't! As long as you have the feather, she'll be in your power. Command her to carry you across the river.'

Jack thanked the ancient woman and climbed onto the back of the horse.

The ball of thread again – whoosh!

So fast, the breath was gone from his body.

They left behind all farms, fields, all signs of humankind. Only rolling hills, green rivers and

frowning mountains. They came to a lake wrapped in mist. Jack hid himself and his horse in a copse of trees and set himself to watch the horizon. Three scars appeared above the lake. They came closer. He saw them to be three fine swans. They flew to the shore, where they shook off their feathers and began to bathe. If the swans were fine, Jack thought the women far finer. Two of them were lovely. The third, the youngest, was beautiful.

While their backs were turned, Jack crept out of the copse and stole a feather. When the women returned to the shore, two of them put on their feathers and flew away. The third took a little longer. She was left behind. She scrabbled among the rocks around her and gave a wail.

Jack stepped forward. 'I have your feather. I'll give it to you if you only carry me across to your father's castle.'

Daughter Greengown turned away. 'I have no father,' she said. 'There is no castle. Return what is mine.'

'Only when you agree to take me to your father.'

Daughter Greengown burst into tears. She put her face in her hands. Her shoulders shook. She sobbed. 'Please, Jack, I beg of you. Have I ever harmed you? Don't punish me for my father's cruelty.'

Jack was overwhelmed with pity. He was filled with shame to have caused such misery. 'Here, take it.'

Daughter Greengown was astonished. She plucked the feather from his hand. 'Many young men have come here, under the spell of my father. Many have tried this trick. But none has ever given me back my feather. You were willing to sacrifice your life for the sake of my happiness. I swear I will help you.'

She pulled on her feathers and became a swan again. Jack climbed onto her back. She beat the air with her wings. They lifted into the mist. Across the lake they went. They passed the trunk of a branchless tree that rose into the fog above them.

Then Jack saw an island, a great green hill rising from the misty lake. And on the hill a castle, wrapped in ivy and brambles and moss.

Daughter Greengown landed on the shore. She became a woman again, kissed Jack and was gone.

Jack waited a while then went to the green castle. The gate was open. There were no servants, no sentrics. There was no sound except the sharpening of an axe. Jack entered the leaf-laden courtyard, and there was the Green Man, rubbing a whetstone against the blade. He looked up.

His green eyes bulged.

His face went the colour of a lime. 'You have found my castle! One of my daughters has helped you.'

'Your daughters?' said Jack. 'I know nothing of your daughters.'

'You lie. Tonight I will keep watch over my eldest daughter. There is another task you must perform. Follow me.'

He led Jack to the stables. As they came closer, Jack could hear a buzzing. When they came closer still, he saw clouds of shiny flies. He saw hills of stinking manure. And the smell! The smell would have made a stone crumble. Disgusting!

'All you have to do is clear out these stables by tomorrow. But if you fail . . . I'll have your head!'

'Is that all? You think it will be hard, but it will be easy.'

And the Green Man was gone.

Jack set to work with a will, but it was no use. The more he shovelled, the greater the task seemed. At last, when his shirt was clinging to his back with sweat, Jack threw down the shovel and wept.

'What is the matter?'

Jack opened his eyes. There was Daughter Greengown.

'What do you think? Unless I clear all this filth

from the stables by tomorrow, your father will have my head.'

'You were kind to me; let me be kind to you. Go inside the castle and sleep. Leave everything to me.'

Jack went to bed, but he couldn't sleep. Not a sound did he hear all night, until the sun rose and he heard the sharpening of an axe. He went down to the courtyard. The Green Man looked up from his blade. He grinned.

'Follow me,' said Jack.

They went to the stables.

Spotless. Not a mark, a stain to be seen.

The Green Man's eyes bulged. He ground his green teeth.

'One of my daughters has helped you!'

'Your daughters? I know nothing of your daughters.'

'Enough! Tonight I will keep watch over my middle daughter. There is another task you must perform. You see that forest? On the farthest shore? You must swim to it and fell every tree by tomorrow. And if you don't . . . I'll have your head!'

'Is that all? You think it will be hard, but it will be easy.'

'I'll see you in the courtyard tomorrow.' With that, the Green Man was gone.

Jack didn't even have an axe. And he couldn't swim. He sat down and put his head in his hands.

'What's the matter?' There was Daughter Greengown again.

'What's the matter? I must swim to that forest and fell every tree by the morning. And if I don't, he'll cut off my head!'

She put her arm on his shoulder. 'When I was in your power, you showed me kindness, so I will return that kindness. Go to your room. Leave the task to me.'

So all day Jack lay on his bed. He heard no sound, no hacking, chopping or sawing, until the sun rose. Then he heard the sharpening of an axe.

He went to the courtyard. There stood the Green Man.

'Follow me,' said Jack.

They climbed to the brambled battlements and looked. They saw a flat plain. No tree to be seen. Not even a stump.

The Green Man's eyes bulged.

He ground his green teeth. 'One of my daughters has helped you!'

'Your daughters?' said Jack. 'I know nothing of your daughters.'

'Enough! Tonight I will keep watch over my youngest daughter. There is another task you must perform. In the lake there is an island. On the island grows one tree. In the tree there is a nest. It is guarded by an eagle. You must fetch me the egg from under the eagle by tomorrow morning. And if you fail . . . I'll have your head!'

'Is that all? You think it will be hard, but it will be easy.'

And the Green Man was gone.

Jack waited until Daughter Greengown appeared.

He told her his task.

'My father is afraid now. If this is the only task he can give you to perform, he must be desperate. My father will be watching for me in the sky. I can't fly to the tree. Come with me.'

They went to the shore.

'Give me your shoe.'

Jack took it off.

'Make a wish. Tell it to be a boat.'

The shoe became a boat. Into the mist they went. They came to the tall tree they'd passed on the way. The trunk was smooth. Not a single branch to help Jack climb. She said, 'Wish my fingers and toes were a ladder.'

Jack wished, and her fingers were gone from her hands, the toes from her feet. He saw a ladder leaning against the tree trunk.

'Careful as you climb and careful with the egg. It is very precious,' she said.

Jack was off, climbing into the mist as carefully as he could, further and further, higher and higher. He saw the nest. In the nest he saw a fierce eagle. Jack shouted, 'Give me that egg!'

The eagle lifted its head and said, 'Jack, don't you remember me? We met long ago. I am the slave of the Green Man. Take the egg. End my misery.'

Jack grabbed the egg.

Now he had to climb down using only one hand, for with the other he held the egg. Out of the mist came two swans, hissing and pecking at his face.

Jack kicked at them and lost his footing. He fell. As he tumbled head over heels, he saw the ladder beside him. He reached and grabbed a rung. He heard a scream from below. When he touched solid ground, he found Daughter Greengown clutching her left foot. Jack had broken her little toe.

They went back to the Green Man's castle.

The Green Man's eyes bulged.

He ground his green teeth.

'So it was Daughter Greengown who betrayed me! She loves you and you love her. Daughter, you will stay with me until the morning. Then you and your sisters will fly over this island as swans. If Jack chooses you from your sisters, then the two of you are free. But if Jack fails, I'll have his head. Jack, I'll see you in the courtyard tomorrow.'

All night Jack lay alone and did not sleep. Next morning he went to the courtyard. There was the Green Man sharpening his axe. Jack heard the beating of wings. The three sisters flew overhead as swans. They were identical – except one of them had a broken claw on her left foot.

Jack pointed. There was Daughter Greengown beside him.

The Green Man's eyes bulged. He ground his green teeth.

'Jack, give me the egg you fetched from the eagle.'

Daughter Greengown said, 'Jack, if you do, he'll cut off your head!'

'Jack, if you don't,' said the Green Man, 'I'll cut off your head. Give me the egg!'

'Jack, that egg is my father's soul!'

'Take it!' Jack threw the egg.

It broke on the Green Man's forehead.

He fell at once. Greengown's sisters wailed.

At their feet they saw flowers bursting out of the cobblestones, forming the shape of a man.